This book belongs to

....

Paws off!
This book belongs to ME!

For all my family and friends –
especially the children in my life and
those eternally young at heart!

Tiger's Eye
Copyright©2022 by Allison Parkinson
Published by Tiger's Eye Books

www.tigerseyebooks.co.uk

Cover and formatting: Stephen Shillito
First paperback print edition: 2022 in the United Kingdom

The right of Allison Parkinson to be identified as
the author and illustrator of this book has been asserted.

No part of this book may be reproduced, stored in a retrieval system,
or transmitted, in any form or by any means, electronic,
mechanical, photocopying, recording or otherwise,
without the prior permission of the author.

ISBN: 978-1-9161948-6-1

Tiger's Eye

Written and illustrated by Allison Parkinson

www.tigerseyebooks.co.uk

Another dawn, the world awakes,
the jungle creatures start to stir.
While, slow and calm, the river runs
its fingers through my fur.

Green waters part at my command,
revealing depths of Indian ink.
The water's cool, it smells so sweet,
I lick my lips, it's time to drink.

My, you must be thirsty,
lapping litres with that tongue so pink.
Look, it's me! Remember me?
We met last week. You do, I think!

Confound your senseless chatter,
you've turned my water sour!
Be off with you or you shall feel
the force of my dread glower!

Ooh, what gorgeous eyes you have,
like discs of burning gold.
You're such a handsome tiger,
with your stripes so dark and bold.

Then tremble at my greatness
as you find yourself before...
Your prince – the most magnificent
Zarif of Jaipurrrr!

You are a noisy fellow!
You just love to make a din,
sitting there as proud as punch,
with your four big paws
and your furry chin.

My chin denotes nobility.
I'm glad you like my paws,
for they hide inside a secret:
four fine sets of...
FEARSOME CLAWS!

I'd love to rub that tummy
and scratch behind your ears.
I could just sit and watch you
for hours, for months – for years!

Then watch how
my tail flicks
and taps a message
just for you.
You've out stayed
your welcome,
so buzz off! Scarper!
Leave my zoo!

The twilight wakes my senses.
Soon the moon will rise
and I will stalk the shadows
and take prey by surprise.

I'll slink down from a tree branch,
or pounce from up on high.

You will not hear me coming.
Like a comet, I shall fly!

Cooee, hello, it's me again!
I was just passing by,
I thought I'd come and sit with you
'till the sun fades from the sky.

Must you spoil my evening
with your loud, incessant shrieking?
How can a Prince go hunting
when you just won't stop speaking?

I want to say I'm sorry that
you're exiled in this zoo.
You're in beautiful surroundings
and they take great care of you.

But you deserve to live your
life away from prying eyes,
in distant lands of green and gold
with never-ending skies.

Bravo! Well said. Now run along
and practice what you preach.
I admire your sheer persistence
but I can't abide your screech.

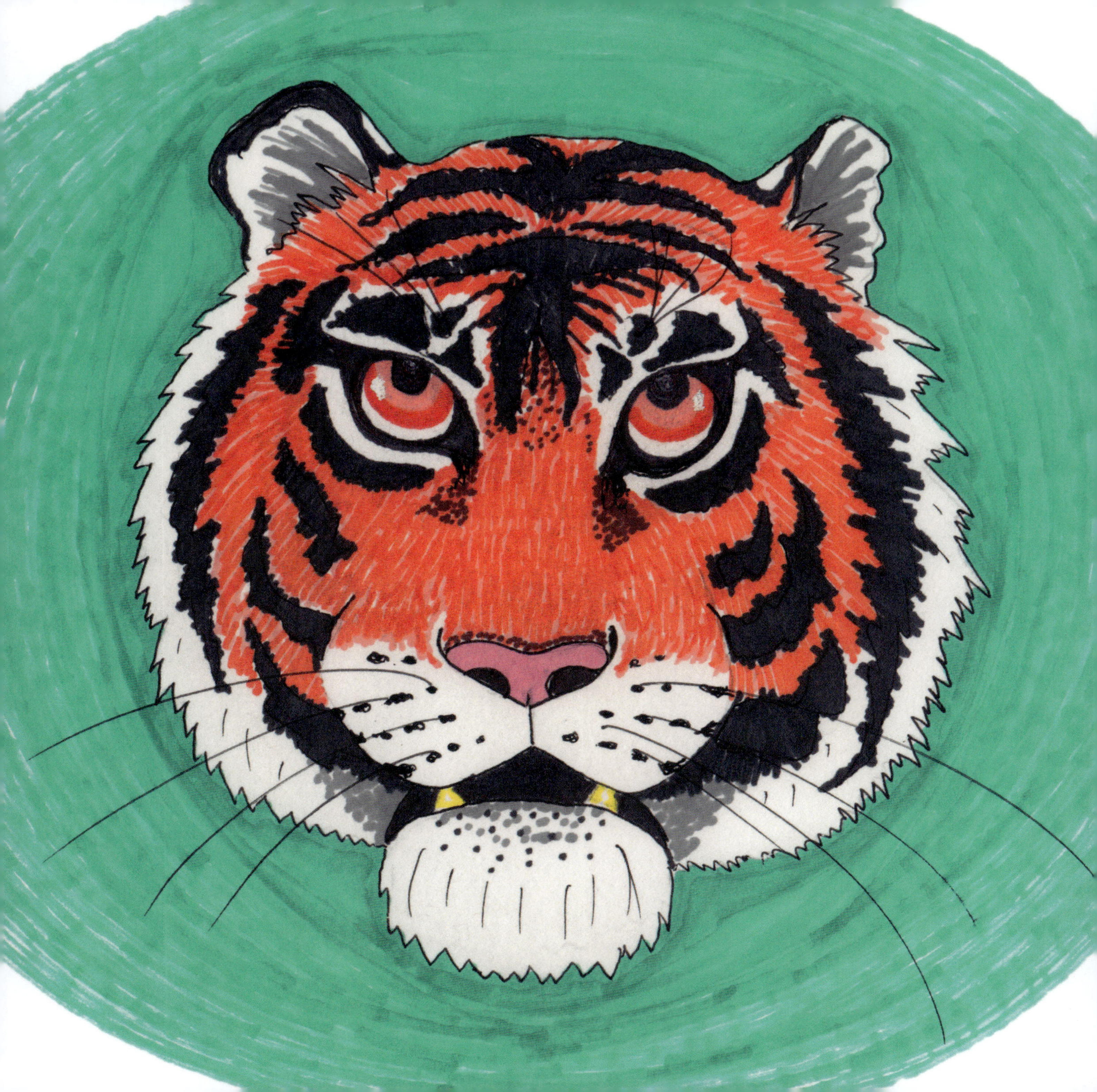

I'm sorry that we humans
have been selfish and so cruel.

But lots of us are just like me,
we think that tigers rule!

The more I see your power
beauty dignity and poise,
the more I want to stand up tall
and make a bloomin' noise!

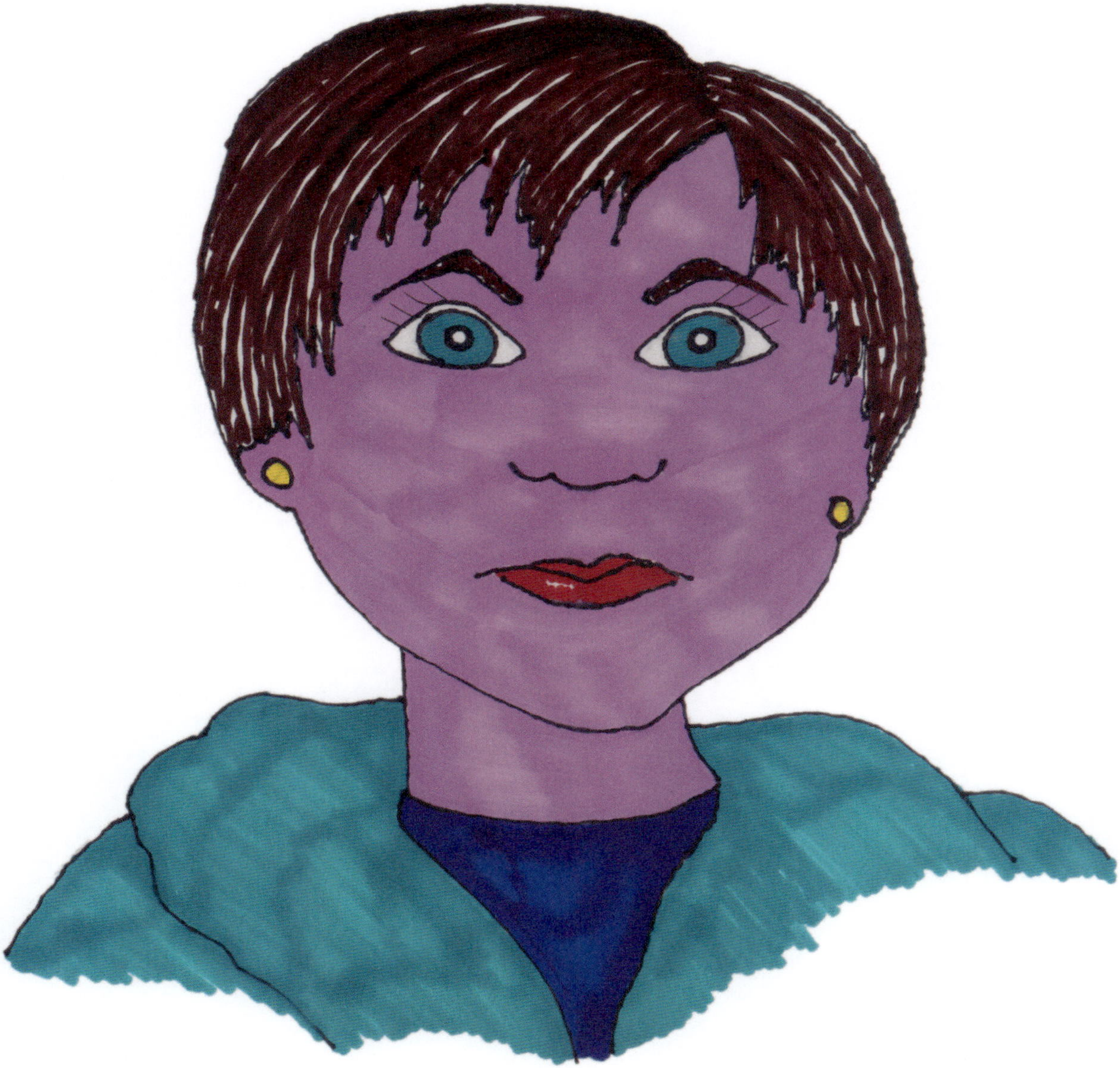

Your face has gone quite purple
and your eyes pop like a toad.
I think that you should calm yourself.
I fear you might explode!

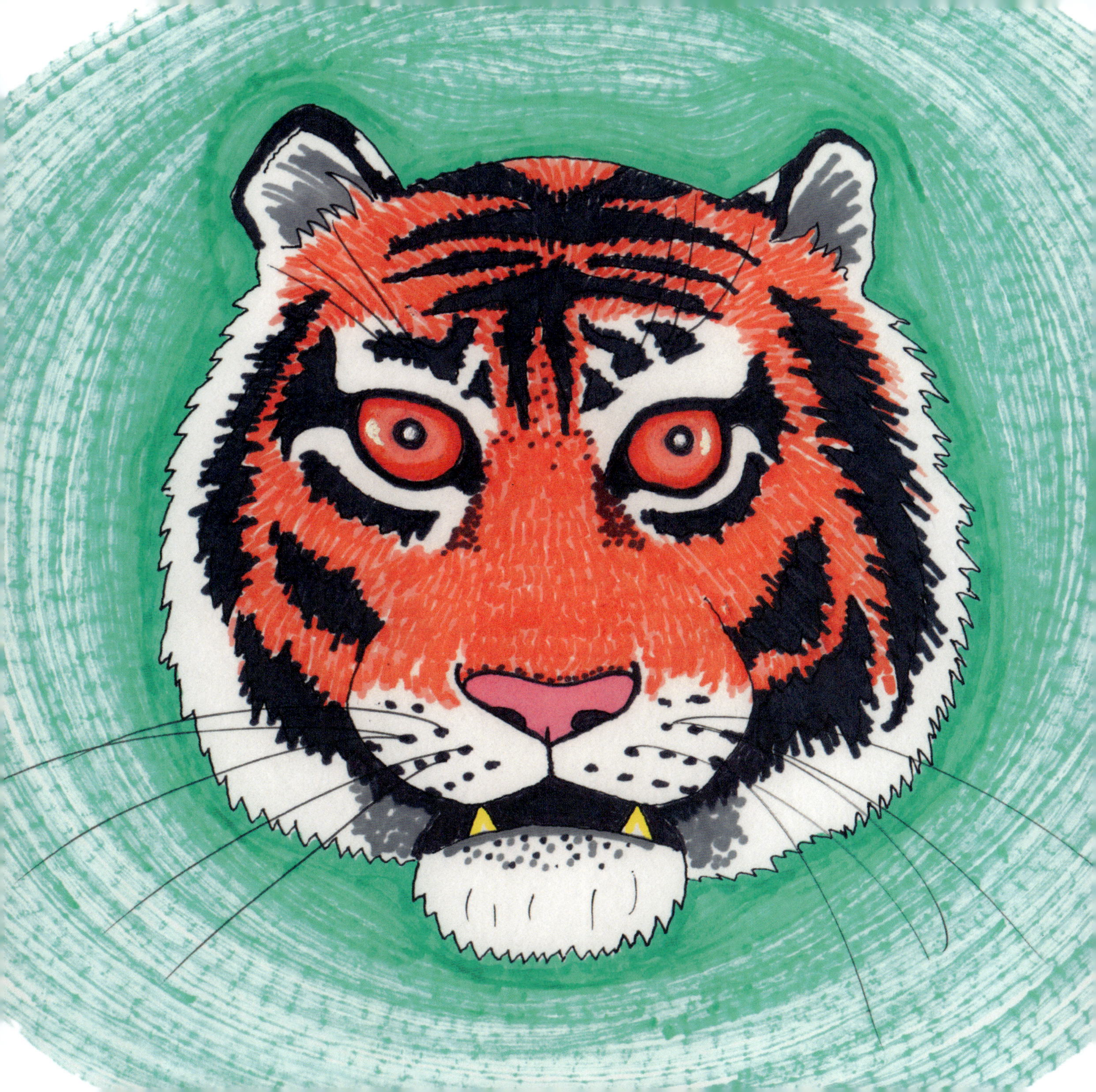

I'm not an angry person,
but I can hold it in no more.
I want to be... a tiger!
I really need to...

ROARRRR!

Well, that was unexpected,
you gave me quite a start...
But now I see the true you —
you have a tiger's heart!

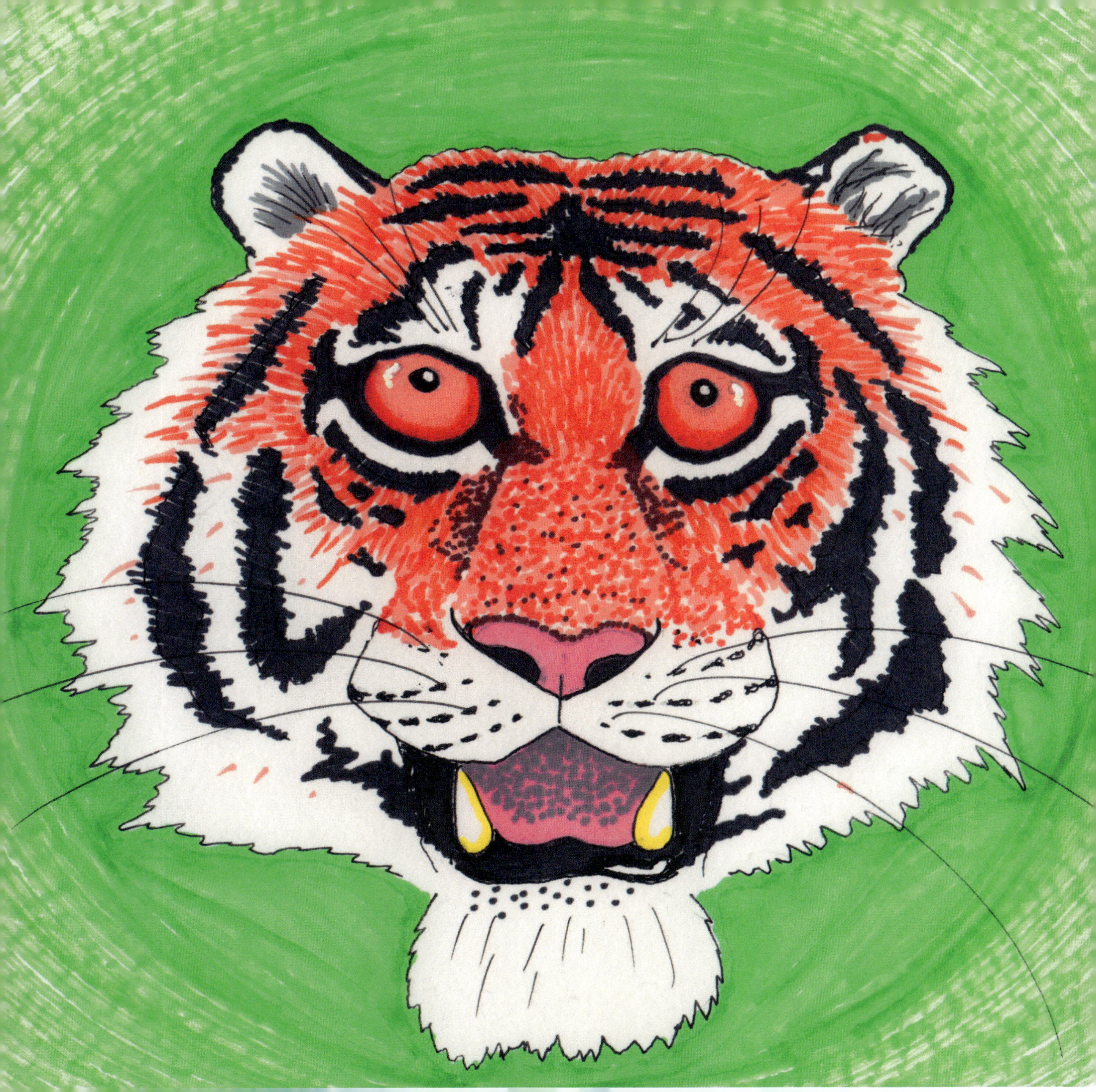

Your chatter still annoys me,
but I'll grant you leave to stay.
And give you royal permission
to visit me each day!

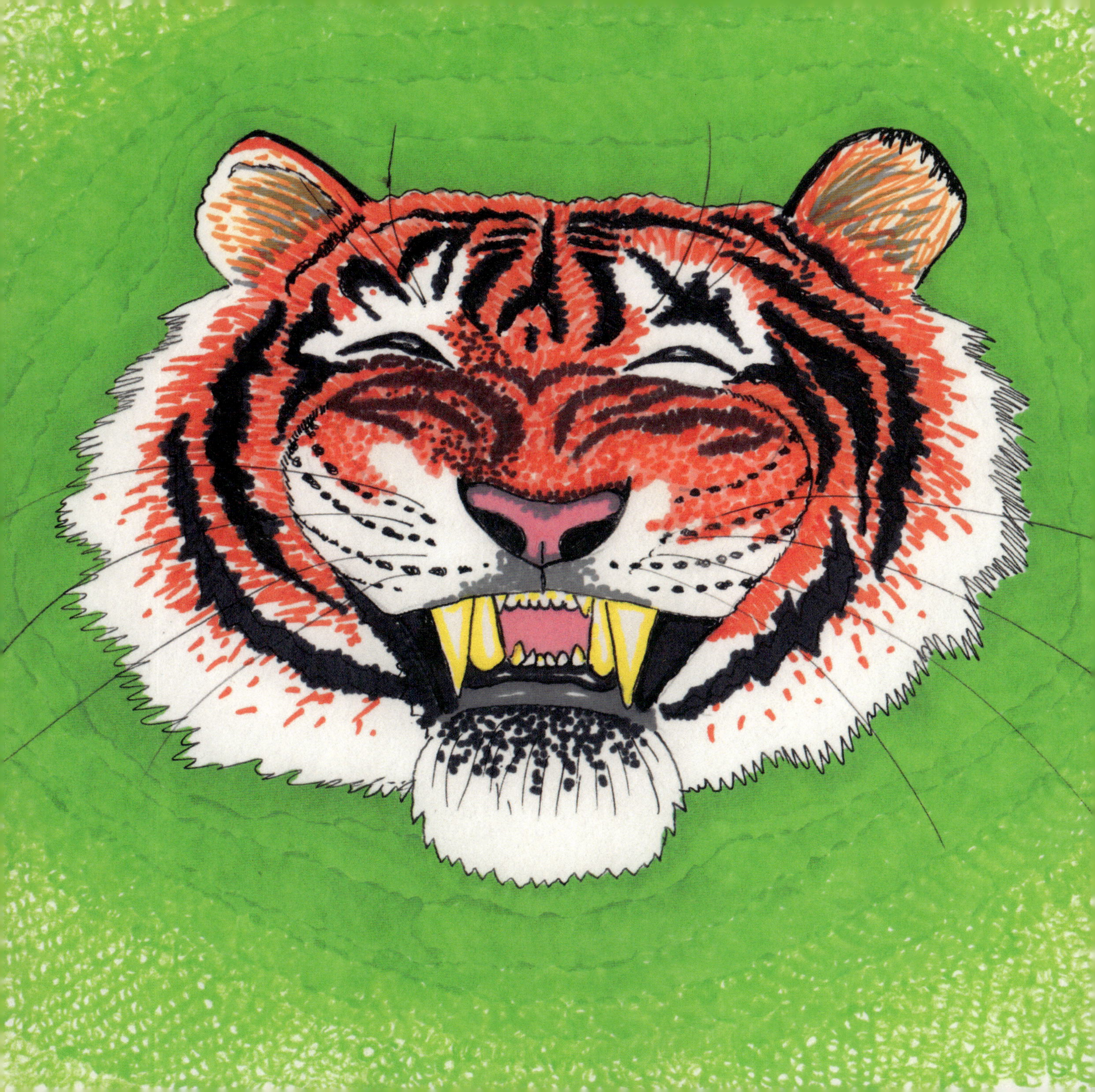

I hope you enjoyed my story!

Zarif and the cat-loving lady first met in my book Tiger Tale. I wanted to bring them back together again because I knew she had something important to say to him – and I wanted them to become good friends.

Talking brings us all closer together so, if you have something important to say, don't bottle it up or be put off by what others may say or think. Take a deep breath, say it out load and – if necessary – be sure to ROAR! Allison x

Of course you enjoyed MY story!

Now hear MY words of wisdom. Around the world, humans just like you are helping my brothers and sisters through organisations such as the WWF **(wwf.org.uk)**. This pleases your Prince greatly. Keep up the good work.

Now you may leave!

Tiger tale
Allison Parkinson

> Magical and mighty... a delightful, roaring tale that my son has learned by heart! Lovely vivid language and a wonderful journey for young souls... a sequel, please!

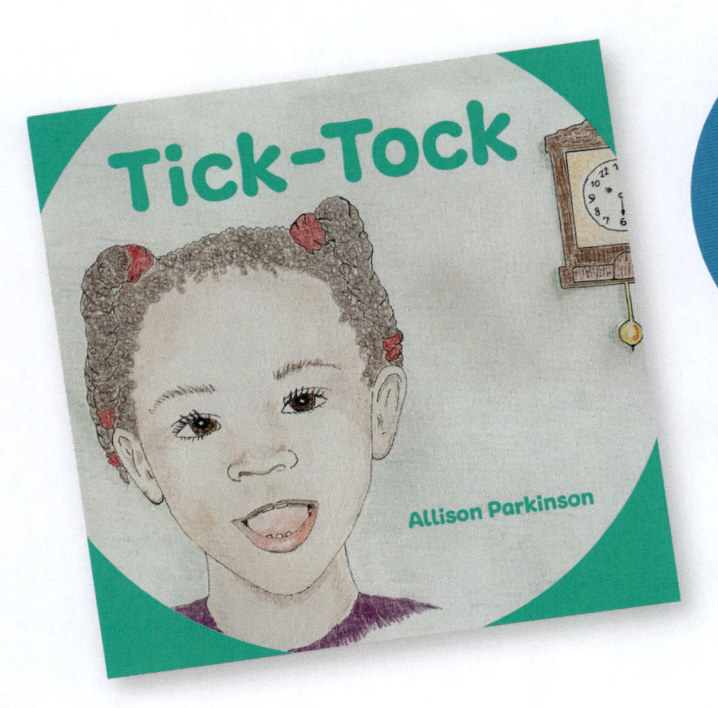

Tick-Tock
Allison Parkinson

> I bought Tick-Tock for my 18 month old niece who unwrapped the paper in which it was hidden, grabbed the book with glee and, having heard an adult say the title, immediately tried to mimic the words, 'Tick-Tock'. This was amazing for one so young. She adored the book.

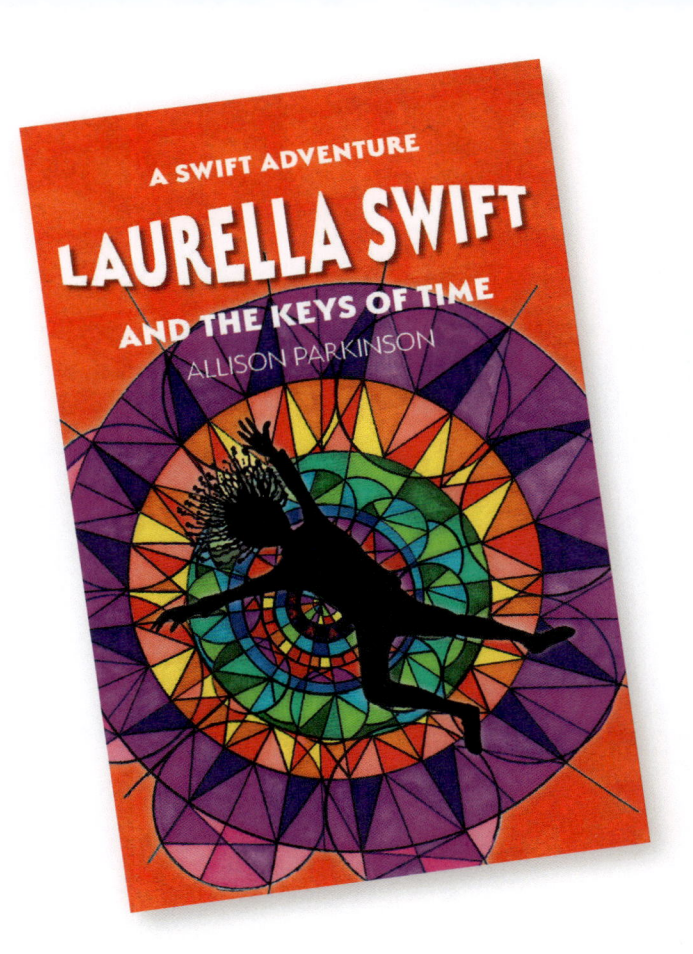

A SWIFT ADVENTURE
LAURELLA SWIFT AND THE KEYS OF TIME
ALLISON PARKINSON

> I like Laurella. She's a fiesty character who is more than equal to the time travelling adventures she finds herself on. She's inquisitive, smart, adaptable, imaginative, darned brave and a great role model.

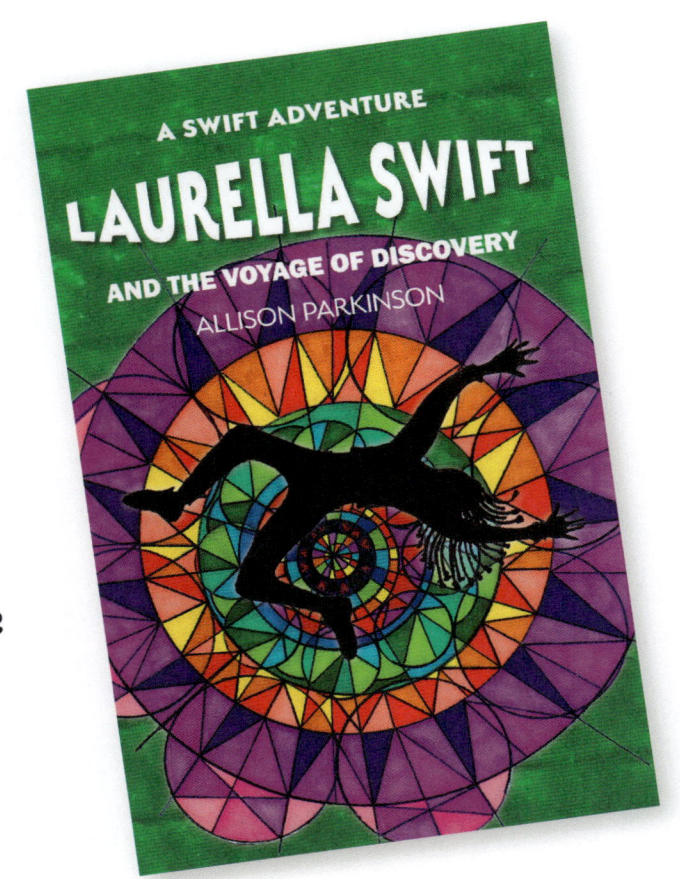

A SWIFT ADVENTURE
LAURELLA SWIFT AND THE VOYAGE OF DISCOVERY
ALLISON PARKINSON

You can find out more about me and my other books at
www.tigerseyebooks.co.uk

Printed in Great Britain
by Amazon